Time Goes By

# A Year in a
# Castle

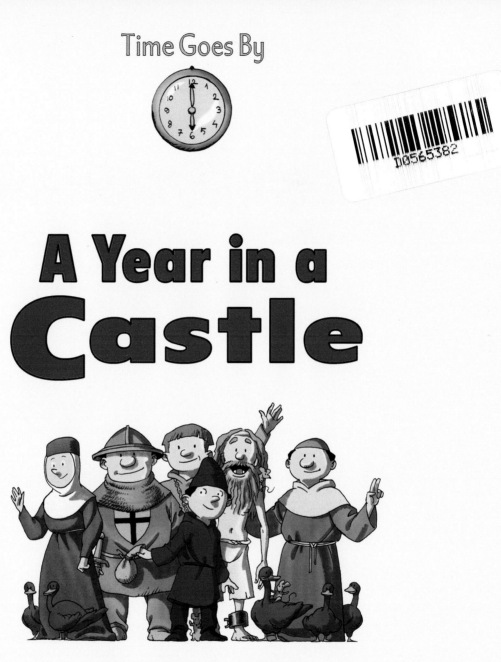

Rachel Coombs

M Millbrook Press / Minneapolis

**First American edition published in 2009 by Lerner Publishing Group, Inc.**

Copyright © 2007 by Orpheus Books Ltd.

Millbrook Press
A division of Lerner Publishing Group, Inc.
241 First Avenue North
Minneapolis, MN  55401 U.S.A.

Website address: www.lernerbooks.com


Library of Congress Cataloging-in-Publication Data

Coombs, Rachel.
   A year in a castle / by Rachel Coombs. — 1st American ed..
     p.   cm. -- (Time goes by)
   Includes bibliographical references.
     ISBN 978–1–58013–550–4 (lib. bdg. : alk. paper)
   1. Castles—Juvenile literature.  2. Civilization, Medieval—Juvenile literature.  I. Title.
GT3550.C66 2009
940.1—dc22                                                    2007048918

Manufactured in the United States of America

5 — BP — 6/1/13

# Table of Contents

# THIS IS THE STORY of

a year in a castle. All the pictures have the same view. But each one shows a different time of year. Lots of things happen during this year. Can you spot them all?

**S**ome pictures have parts of the walls taken away. This helps you see inside the castle.

**Y**ou can follow all the action at the castle as the months pass. The calendar on each right-hand page tells you what month it is.

**A**s you read, look for people that appear every month. For example, keep an eye on the lord and lady of the castle. They are very busy. And look out for a prisoner. He's always up to something! Can you spot the thief? Think about what stories these people might tell about life in the castle.

Can you
find . . .

a guard?

**A** new castle has just been built. The lord and his family are moving in. All over the castle, people unpack. The inner bailey is a courtyard inside the castle walls. A cart has collapsed there. It was carrying too many grain sacks. A water-filled moat, or ditch, goes around the castle. Guards laugh as a man swims in it!

a priest?

a well?

It's market day at the castle. Local people come to buy food. Musicians, a stilt walker, and a sword swallower perform for the people. Inside the castle, the lord greets his cousin who has come to visit. The cousin wants his daughter to marry the lord's son. He has brought expensive gifts. In the chapel, a priest tries to teach a class of children. But they aren't paying much attention!

March

Moving in

**Market day**

Tournament

Feasting

Attack!

The siege continues

Making repairs

Christmas

Can you find . . .

a hawk?

a knight?

The lord's son is getting married. So the lord holds a contest called a tournament. He has invited knights from across the land. The knights gather at the back of the castle. They carry lances and try to knock one another off their horses. Some knights get injured. In the inner bailey, knights shoot arrows at targets. In the kitchen, the servants decorate a cake.

April

Moving in

Market day

**Tournament**

Feasting

Attack!

The siege continues

Making repairs

Christmas

Can you
find . . .

a jester?

the lord and lady?

a horse
and carriage?

A huge feast is taking place in the largest room in the castle. The room is called the Great Hall. The lord and lady sit at the head of the table. Jesters and acrobats entertain the guests. The kitchen is busy. The cooks prepare all the food. The servants rush the food across the inner bailey to serve the guests. Upstairs, the maids try on the lady's clothes.

## Can you find . . .

a catapult?

a bow and arrow?

a battering ram?

a fainting maid?

**A**n enemy lord attacks the castle! Guards raise the drawbridge. Some help put out fires. They shoot arrows at the enemy. Inside the walls, the servants train to defend the castle. In the Great Hall, guards tell the lord what is happening. A few enemy soldiers have sneaked into the kitchen. The servants fight them.

## Can you find . . .

an injured man?

a flaming arrow?

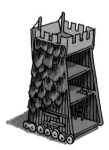

a rescue?

a belfry?

The attack continues. It is a siege—an attack that lasts many months. The guards have put wooden planks around the walls. The planks help protect the castle. But enemy soldiers fire burning arrows. The soldiers try to climb over the walls using a tall wooden tower. Inside, the castle is running out of food. Many guards are injured. The Great Hall has been turned into a hospital.

August

Moving in

Market day

Tournament

Feasting

Attack!

**The siege continues**

Making repairs

Christmas

## Can you find . . .

builders?

a man fixing
the roof?

a maid sweeping?

a knighting
ceremony?

**T**he siege is over at last. The guards have finally defeated the enemy! The lord rewards the bravest fighters by making them knights. But he thinks others might be stealing from him. A trial takes place. Those found guilty are put in prison. Workers begin to repair the castle.

October

Moving in

Market day

Tournament

Feasting

Attack!

The siege continues

Making repairs

Christmas

Can you
find . . .

some geese?

children skating?

guards
warming up?

a snowman?

a play?

**T**he lord holds a Christmas feast. He invites some of the local farmers. A few are very greedy! Upstairs, the lady catches the thief. Outside, actors perform a Christmas play. Some children (and some guards!) build snowmen. One guard notices the prisoner has escaped! The first year in the castle has been busy. Will next year be just as busy?

December

Moving in

Market day

Tournament

Feasting

Attack!

The siege continues

Making repairs

Christmas

# Glossary

**acrobats:** people who perform gymnastic tricks

**battering ram:** a heavy wooden beam, sometimes protected by a hut on wheels. It is rammed against a wall or gate to punch through it.

**belfry:** a tower

**catapult:** a weapon used for firing rocks over castle walls

**drawbridge:** a bridge that can be raised or lowered

**Great Hall:** the largest room in a castle

**inner bailey:** a courtyard inside the castle walls

**jesters:** people hired to make others laugh. Jesters often wear colorful clothing and hats with bells on them.

**knights:** warriors from long ago. Knights worked for important families and protected them.

**moat:** a deep ditch around a castle that is filled with water

**siege:** an attack that lasts many months

**tournament:** a contest for knights

**trial:** examining evidence in a court of law to decide if a person is guilty of a crime

# Learn More about Castles

## Books

Carlson, Laurie M. *Days of Knights and Damsels: An Activity Guide*.
  Chicago: Chicago Review Press, 1998.
Hooper, Meredith. *Stephen Biesty's Castles*. New York: Enchanted Lion
  Books, 2004.
Langley, Andrew. *Castle at War: The Story of a Siege*. New York: DK Pub., 1998.
MacDonald, Fiona. *How to Be a Medieval Knight*. Washington, DC: National Geographic, 2005.
Murrell, Deborah Jane, *The Best Book of Knights and Castles*. Boston: Kingfisher, 2005.
Steer, Dugald. *Knight: A Noble Guide for Young Squires*. Cambridge, MA: Candlewick Press, 2006.

## Websites

Castle Learning Center
http://www.castles-of-britain.com/castle6.htm
Find out more about building castles, living in castles, and knights. A parent or teacher can help
read and explain the information on this site.

Castles for Kids
http://www.castles.org/Kids_Section/Castle_Story/index.htm
This website gives names for all the parts of a castle and also tells about many of the people who
worked at castles.

Destroy the Castle
http://www.pbs.org/wgbh/nova/lostempires/trebuchet/destroy.html
Play this game using a weapon called a trebuchet to destroy a castle. The website also includes
more winformation about sieges.

# A Closer Look

This book has a lot to find. Did you see people who showed up again and again? Think about what these people did and saw during the year. If these people kept journals, what would they write? A journal is a book with blank pages where people write down their thoughts. Have you ever kept a journal? What did you write about?

Try making a journal for one of the characters in this book. You will need a pencil and a piece of paper. Choose your character. Give your character a name. Write the name of the month at the top of the page. Underneath, write about the character's life during that month. Pretend you are the character. What do you do all day long? Is your life hard or easy? Why? What have you noticed about the other people at the castle? Have you seen anything surprising? What? What do you hope to do next month?

Don't worry if you don't know how to spell every word. You can ask a parent or teacher for help if you need to. And be creative!

# Index